THIS BOOK BELONGS TO:

_____

For David and Paul

This paperback edition first published in 2018 by Andersen Press Ltd.
First published in Great Britain in 2017 by Andersen Press Ltd.,
20 Vauxhall Bridge Road, London SW1V 2SA.
Copyright © Ciara Flood, 2017.
The right of Ciara Flood to be identified as the author and
illustrator of this work has been asserted by her in accordance
with the Copyright, Designs and Patents Act, 1988.
All rights reserved.
Printed and bound in China.

1 3 5 7 9 10 8 6 4 2

British Library Cataloguing in Publication Data available.
ISBN 978 1 78344 587 5

Ciara Flood

There's a
WALRUS
in My Bed!

Ⓐ

Andersen Press

Flynn was very excited about sleeping in his new bed.

But there was one rather large problem.

"Mum, Dad, there's a walrus in my bed," said Flynn.

"You must have been dreaming," said Dad.

"But there really, really is!"

"You know it's naughty to tell fibs," said Mum.

Flynn sighed and went back to his bedroom.

Flynn was trying to squeeze into the bed when he heard a very loud noise coming from Walrus' tummy.

ruumM

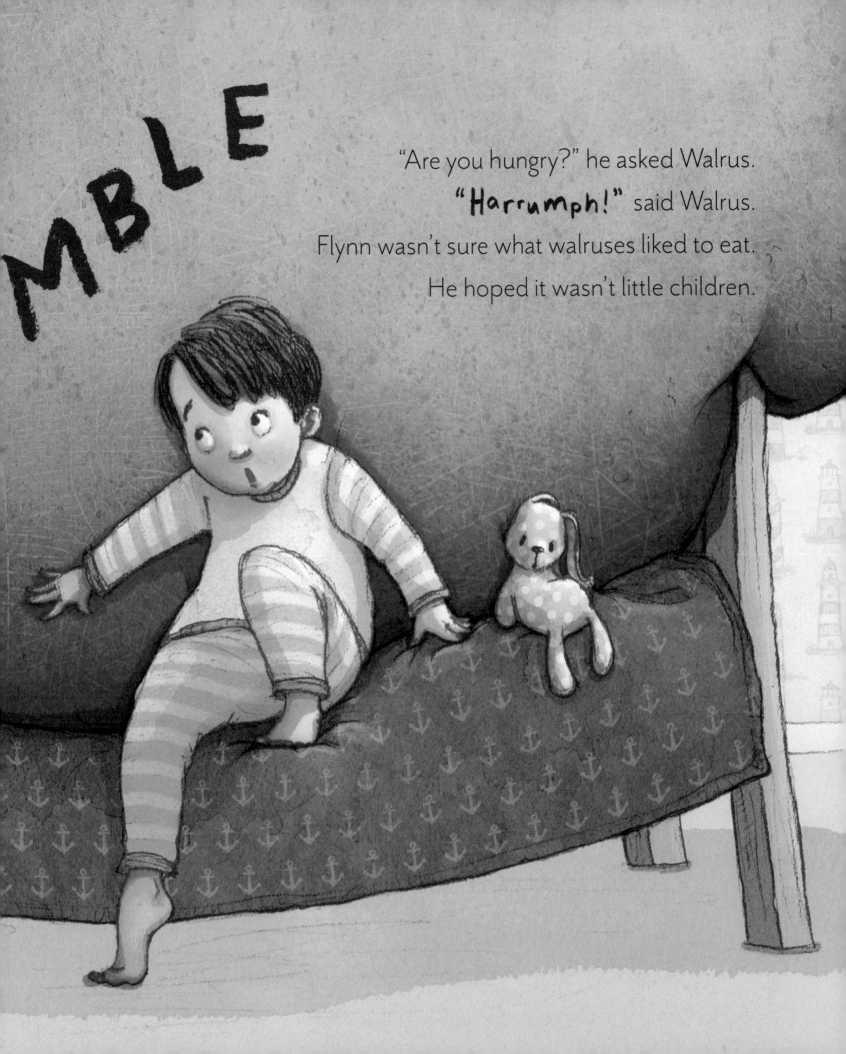

MBLE

"Are you hungry?" he asked Walrus.

"Harrumph!" said Walrus.

Flynn wasn't sure what walruses liked to eat.

He hoped it wasn't little children.

"Flynn, it's far too late
for snacks," said Mum.
"But they're not for me,
they're for Walrus," Flynn told her.

Walrus ate all the snacks.
He didn't seem hungry any more,
but he wasn't sleepy either.

"ACHOOO!"

sneezed Walrus.

"Do you have a cold?" Flynn asked.
"Harrumph!" sniffed Walrus.

Flynn got some extra blankets.

Walrus started to get hot and cranky.

"Oh dear," said Flynn.

"You must be really sick."

"Harrumph!"

wheezed Walrus.

"Walrus isn't feeling well – he needs
a glass of milk," said Flynn.
"Perhaps Walrus shouldn't have eaten
all those snacks," Dad muttered.

After drinking the milk,

Walrus had to use the bathroom.

"I know you're a little nervous about your new bed,"

said Mum, "but it's way past your bedtime."

"It's not me who won't go to sleep,"

grumbled Flynn. "It's Walrus!"

"OK, Walrus, that's enough messing around!" said Flynn. "I'm going to sing you to sleep."
"Harrumph!" said Walrus, who still looked wide awake.

"Are you scared of monsters?"

"Harrumph!"

"Or do you have an itch you can't reach?"

Flynn had a long, hard think.

"Maybe what you really need is..."

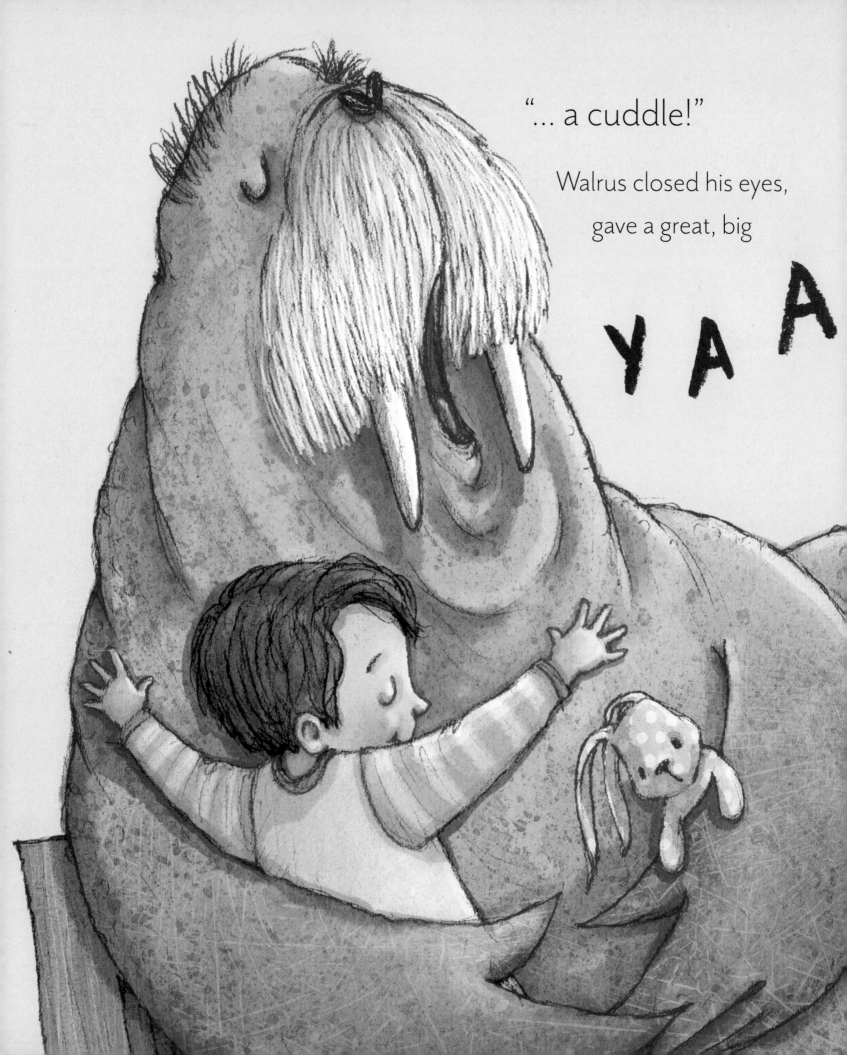

"... a cuddle!"

Walrus closed his eyes,
gave a great, big

YAA

A A W W N

and finally fell asleep.

Flynn snuggled down beside him.

But there was still one rather large problem...

 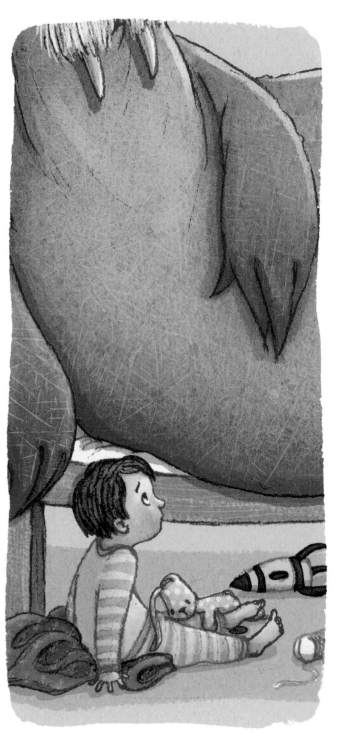

the bed just wasn't big enough for both of them.
Flynn tiptoed into Mum and Dad's bedroom.

"Mum, Dad," he whispered,
"can Walrus sleep in your bed tonight?"
"If we say yes will you promise to go
to sleep?" asked Mum. Flynn nodded.
"Yes!!" they both shouted.

Flynn stretched out in his soft, warm bed.
"Night night, Walrus," he said.
"Harrumph!" said Walrus.

And at last everyone could go to sleep.

Well, almost everyone.